# VeggieTales

## Saint Nicholas

### A Veggie Christmas Story

**Adapted by Karen Poth**
**Illustrated by John Trauscht**

Based on the VeggieTales video *Saint Nicholas: A Veggie Christmas Story*

🌱 **A GOLDEN BOOK • NEW YORK**

www.randomhouse.com/kids
Library of Congress Control Number: 2008942405     ISBN: 978-0-375-85722-5
Printed in the United States of America
10 9 8 7 6 5 4 3 2 1

It was the day before Christmas. Everyone in town was shopping, decorating, and running errands. Junior was busy finishing up his list for Santa when a question popped into his head.

"If Christmas is when we celebrate the birth of Jesus," Junior asked, "what does Saint Nicholas have to do with that?"

"That's a great question," Bob the Tomato said. Junior, Annie, Laura, and Jimmy got quiet as Bob told them this story.

A long, long time ago, in a faraway place called Greece, there lived a fisherman named Epiphanus. He was known as a kind man who was happy to share what he had with others.

Epiphanus had a son named Nicholas. The boy loved his parents and his home and his friend Octavius. But most of all, he loved fishing with his father.

One night, while Nicholas and his father were fishing, a huge ship pulled into port. Gustav, the ship's captain, handed his tired workers their wages as they left the ship.

"This is not enough to feed my family," said one worker.

"That is too bad!" shouted the stingy Gustav, pushing the man along.

Epiphanus felt sorry for the worker. "If it's food you need, knock on my door," he said. "You will not leave hungry."

Later that night, Nicholas asked his father, "If we give away our fish, will I have to work for Gustav?"

"No," his father replied. "God has blessed us with much. Don't worry! When you're grown up and I am gone, our boats will belong to you."

It wasn't long before his parents were gone, and Nicholas was left alone to take care of his father's fishing business. The townsfolk came to Nicholas for fish to feed their families. But there were too many people!

"I can't do this without my father!" Nicholas
said to Octavius. "I'm leaving!"

Nicholas climbed aboard a fishing boat and set sail. He wasn't sure where he was going. He just wanted to get away from his troubles. Octavius was sad to see his friend go.

Nicholas spent many years sailing from port to port. Finally, he came to the city of Bethlehem. Nicholas remembered that his father had told him it was the place where Jesus was born.

As Nicholas walked through Bethlehem, he saw a woman feeding the poor. "God loves you," she said as each grateful person left her table. "Go in peace."

"Why are you doing this?" Nicholas asked. "Does it make you happy?"

"I do it because I *am* happy," the woman replied. "My love is a gift to them, just as God's son was a gift to me."

For the first time, Nicholas realized that his parents had given to others because God had given to them.

"It is time for me to go home and finish my parents' work!" Nicholas shouted.

When Nicholas got home, everything was different. Gustav was the mayor. He owned every booth in the marketplace and every store on the square. Gustav had left the townsfolk with nothing.

As Nicholas stood there, he read Gustav's latest decree.

ANYONE CAUGHT GIVING A GIFT TO ANOTHER WILL PAY A FINE OF ONE GOLD COIN. IF THEY CANNOT PAY, THEY WILL BE THROWN IN JAIL — FOREVER!

"This is terrible!" Nicholas cried. "How will I ever do my parents' good work if Gustav won't let me give gifts?"

"Remember the words of Jesus," his old friend Octavius said wisely. "When you give to the needy, do not let your left hand know what your right hand is doing."

"That's it!" Nicholas exclaimed. "We will give our gifts in secret."

That night, Nicholas and Octavius slipped out into the city to give gifts. They had put on many different disguises so that no one would know who they were.

Gustav's men were guarding all the doors and windows around town. But that didn't stop Nicholas. He and Octavius jumped quietly from rooftop to rooftop.

"Ho, ho, ho!" Nicholas laughed in his new disguise with his bag of gifts thrown over his shoulder. No matter how hard Gustav's guards looked, they could not find Nicholas.

Nicholas delivered gifts to everyone in need by dropping them down the chimney of each house on his list. After many years, people all over the world began to give gifts on one special night of the year.

"So, just like Nicholas, we can share God's love with others—by giving?" Junior asked when Bob had finished his story.

"I couldn't have said it better myself," said Bob.

"This is the best Christmas ever!" Junior shouted. Everyone agreed, and they began to sing:

*I can love because God loves me,*
*I can give because God gave.*
*Jesus's love is why I'm smiling,*
*Why I'm giving Christmas Day.*